"The poem is a vale of soul-making."

~Sharon Olds

Here
at the Crux

Leanne Boschman

720 – Sixth Street, Box # 5
New Westminster, BC
CANADA   V3C 3C5

Title: Here at the Crux
Author: Leanne Boschman
Publisher: Silver Bow Publishing
Cover Art: "Awry" collage by Edward Epp
Author Photo: Mr & Mrs Smith Studios
Editing: Candice James

www.silverbowpublishing.com
info@silverbowpublishing.com
© silver bow publishing 2022
ISBN 9781774032312 print
ISBN 9781774032329 ebook

Library and Archives Canada Cataloguing in Publication

Title: Here at the crux / Leanne Boschman.
Names: Boschman, Leanne, 1960- author.
Identifiers: Canadiana (print) 20220279020 | Canadiana (ebook) 20220279047 | ISBN 9781774032312
   (softcover) | ISBN 9781774032329 (ebook)
Classification: LCC PS8603.O83 H47 2022 | DDC C811/.6—dc23

5

for Edie and Francis

Contents

PART ONE
The Human Scent

PART TWO
Unsparing Season

PART THREE
Sing Only of Return

PART ONE

The Human Scent

"I would like to go, as at last Bonnard did,
all the way into the world of the living.
To sit there a while in the petals, altering nothing."

from *Heart Stopping and Starting in the Late Dark*
~ Jane Hirshfield

Tuesday's Child

"Tuesday's Child is full of grace" -from a traditional nursery rhyme

The nurse's hands—were they warm
or cold clamps of a vice-grip exacting pressure
as she placed me on the white metal scale?
They were not my mother's hands.
My mother, still shackled after the thrashing,
the amnesia drug—a mix of morphine and scopolamine—
it's unlikely she smiled when the obstetrician,
a little more Marcus Welby than Dr. Kildare with a brisk grin
told her *you have a little girl, Mrs. Boschman.*
My mother slept off the drugs for days, reminded me
for the rest of her life how godawful the whole thing was.

Gleaming placenta-tree in a metal wastebin,
and in the small industrial crib below the gauze-sky
of fluorescent lit ceiling I lay until my father arrived.
Slapped on the back, too, after the news
reached him at a track meet. *Congratulations coach*
echoing behind him as he ran to his car.
He gasped at the sight of my forceps-bruised
misshapen skull, so the nurse reassured him
that baby's heads are malleable, will mend
and be right again, but when she held me out
said *here is your daughter*, my fleet-footed father
stumbled backwards blurted *are you sure?*

He loved to tell this story each year on my birthday
and I still hear it, but now I listen in
for the crinkle of small ice puddles breaking,
the rustle of newly knitted limbs under starched sheets
and birds flying back, navigating by stars,
by waves, by the magnetic field of earth,
the smell of earth opening.
I look for green rosaries of cottonwood seeds
and pussy-willows in prairie twilight sleep
of early April. I begin to hear
the budding benediction of that day.

Late Summer Resurrection

The memory is resurrected
while watching day-time television
through the mind-muffling haze of cold medications—
alarmed-looking boomers find out a childhood virus,
dormant for years in nerve roots, can be reactivated,
erupt through the skin, a kind of viral déjà vu.
Then they're reassured there's a vaccine
for this lingering vulnerability
of childhood's confounding seasons.

Like that summer when I was six
and the big girls next door,
sisters with rhyming names, Judy and Trudy,
held their own vacation Bible school
in an old yellow bus parked in the alley behind their house.
My brother and a few neighbourhood kids
made crosses out of popsicle sticks.
I happily glued, coloured, and savoured the toffees I received
for memorization and warbling Sunday school songs.

On the last day, Judy sent me into their house for more paper.
When I lingered to look at a paint-by-numbers picture
of flamingoes, thin stems of their legs
stuck in a drab olive pond,
their mother appeared,
stood in the kitchen doorway
blocking my exit.
She couldn't sleep, she said.
The pain was like being stabbed with a burning fork.
Light was unbearable.

When she told me she had shingles,
I pictured roof tiles that sometimes blew off in windstorms.
Perhaps because of the confusion narrowing my eyes,
she pulled up her pajama top,
showed me the streak of blistering sores
that stretched from her back across her ribcage,
stopping just below her right breast.

Speechless, I stood on my own stick legs
until she went back to her bedroom, then I ran outside.

I toppled into the last torn vinyl bus-seat,
stared out at the rutted alleyway,
wishing I had a sister whose name rhymed with mine,
who could explain such things.
It was my brother, wearing a straw cowboy hat,
who called into the bus, said everyone was waiting.

For a special treat we dipped rhubarb in sugar
while listening to one more story about Jesus
who touched children gently on their heads,
who healed the sick and multiplied the loaves and fish.

When asked to say a final silent prayer,
my supplication started with LePage's glue bottles—
that they would never run dry,
and that Laurentian pencil crayons, especially my favourites—
Desert Topaz and Sky Magenta—could last
no matter how many times they were sharpened.

Then I prayed fervently for the resurrection of the old bus,
for it to rumble to life so that we could roll out
through ripening wheat fields to Eagle Creek
where we would swim,
shaded by chokecherry bushes and wolf willow,
dragonflies whirring around us.

Finally, I asked that the red stripe
wrapped around Mrs. M.'s pale flesh
would quiver and loosen then flap its wretched wings
into the late summer sunset.

Singing Lessons

At twelve years old I was completely smitten
with Georgia Terry.
She sang wearing a black lace gown, her dark hair
sleeked back in a chignon, but when I begged
to be enrolled in Georgia's music academy,
Mother, you mocked her—arms outstretched
and after some lunatic screeching
said *forget about that diva, I can give you singing lessons.*

Saturday afternoons, you sat with your friends
around our kitchen table where you set out
three square meals a day.
It always started with coffee and cigarettes.
Later *something a little stronger*
and your side-splitting jokes and stories.
Like the one about the quick-tempered manager
whose face turned crimson when his steno pool *girls*
didn't produce a memo quickly enough.
Then he hurled a coffee cup out of his office door,
didn't care whom or what he hit until one day you,
at nineteen, picked it up and casually threw it back.
Nailed him on the shoulder.
And always the one about how at three-years-old,
I sloshed through mud puddles in your tap shoes.
Completely ruined them.

Not long ago, one of your friends sent me
an old home movie—*you'll get a kick out of this.*
There you are at a party in one of your signature
polka dot blouses, the demure clasp of your hands
at the first notes of *O Promise Me.*
But the piano player knows your forte, swings
the tempo and with a toss of your dishevelled hair
and a twirl of the boa,
you take it burlesque and suddenly I appreciate
what I couldn't before—
how you were holding nothing back.

Hymns for Sad Ballads

On weekend mornings Grandma Neufeld,
still in her mauve quilted housecoat, got agitated,
made us turn off Saturday morning cartoons.
I can't recall now if it was coyote or roadrunner
who opened boxes labelled TNT,
ignited countless bundles of red sticks,
but with those loud pops and fizzles silenced,
she said
        You kids just don't know.
        Explosions and gunshots aren't funny.
        They're what kill your neighbors.
Sometimes she followed up her stories
with vocabulary lessons—
        Bolshevik, Menshevik, Kulak, Gulag.

When I told my mother
about the Saturday morning stories, she shrugged.
Grandma Neufeld had a right to her *blue spells*
and tearful reminiscences.
We could never quite keep their names straight—
the family members,
friends she never saw again
after leaving her Mennonite village in Ukraine.

At twenty-one she arrived in Canada
with a husband and one-year old daughter
who weighed no more than a six-month baby,
and that baby, she told us,
was more like a scrawny fledgling,
too weak to even cry.
She stepped onto the train that delivered them at last
to the stark centre of a prairie winter.
Sometime after that, she stopped going to church,
traded hymns for sad ballads.

At fourteen when I was planning to be a folksinger
and played my guitar every morning before school,

she asked me to sing *Four Strong Winds*.
She always wiped away tears
with a crumpled handkerchief when I got to the line
I'll look for you if I'm ever back this way.

To this day my eyes are still convinced they, too,
saw her neighbor.
The way she described him lying there,
a ragdoll with shreds of stuffing
spilling out onto grass.

I sometimes picture her on that last day
promising to return,
buttoning up her coat
before that cold wind blew
through the rest of her life.

What's Down There

What compels them to tell those stories again and again,
my mother and her nine sisters around the table over the years
smoking, drinking coffee, remembering. Stories collect in the
pockets of my memory along with all childhood's jumbled artifacts.
Some are polished smooth, harmless over time: others have sharp
edges that trouble my daydreams.
   When they play dentist, sister Marge pulls out my mother's
tooth with the pliers, makes her promise not to tell, though she is
sputtering, crying, blood running down her chin.
   One evening when sister Ella comes strolling up the front
walk with her date, they open an upstairs window, throw
brassieres and panties down on them.
   Mrs. Schmidt, the librarian always says, *Girls, the balls
of my feet pain me so, they just pain me something terrible.*
Then those girls all run out laughing. *The balls of my feet,
the balls of my feet.*
   On a Sunday afternoon, in the middle of winter, their parents
away, my mother puts on her bathing suit, skates on the frozen
dugout. Snowflakes fall on her dark hair, melt on her skin.
They all cheer and one takes a photograph.
   In a quiet voice, my mother tells how Uncle Henry, not really
their uncle, backs her into the chicken coop. How she tells him,
Bugger off, you old asshole. Then her father spanks her the one
and only time after the so-called uncle reports the young girl
talking like a savage.
   Then there is the night cousin Ericka, three months
pregnant, has a fall down the cellar steps. Wait, I know there
is more to the story, though I can't ask them. There is the dank
smell of the dirt floor, a thud and muffled cry that sends mice
scurrying. Mason jars tremble on crude wooden shelves. Light
glints off the purple of beets and pink crab apples nestled in thick,
rich syrup. There is a heavy feeling in her belly, like a stone
dropping. There are potatoes, all their eyes staring down there
in the dark.

Terrace Revisited

At the Saturday morning farmer's market these runty
northern apples will likely end up sauced.
Cellophane-wrapped butter tarts, bread lined up on folding tables,
hand-knit socks dangle beneath tarps along with waist aprons,
broods of baby bonnets.
Bouquets from Portuguese flowerbeds that brim with red
dahlias, calico asters.

I'm a visitor now to this town, my home not so long ago
but long enough to notice new lines cross-hatched into faces
of women in this amiable living-room—its pocked floor,
photos of teens in grad gowns.
In the drum circle my hands find each beat again, and I'm lulled
awhile by this mid-day rhythm; then after good-byes
surprised by my urge to toss the gift of silver
dollar seeds to the wind and run down back-alleys pitching apples.

Restless Children

Late night passengers on the last sailing
slump into vinyl seats; down the aisles run a few
restless children, parents stumbling after.
Our tired faces reflected in smudged windows,
we barely lift our feet for the vacuum cleaner.
My daughter works grimly on a job application.
I slip into murky sleep, awaken to see the other girl.
Crimson lipstick seems almost black against
her chalky skin in that meager light.
She paces until Vancouver lights appear.
She asks me just before we dock and again just after
if we can give her a lift, but I say *no*
we're not going that way.

Swamped by the wake of my own reckless days,
crazy nights hitchhiking,
suddenly I'm frantic to find that girl.
A panicked search as we leave the terminal
because that girl could have been my own, or me,
just a little lost and who else might see
that look on her face when she asks for a ride.
Deserted parking lot offers no answers.
Empty bus shelters only parentheses of regret.
Still on our way into the city I stare
into the backseat of every car we pass.

Taken

Dark insinuations of probes, ultrasound, x-rays--finally
the week arrives when my mother receives her test results.

Back home a few grey and rust-brown feathers on the deck.
Do birds fly unsuspecting into these windows? Can't help

wondering what that moment would be like: the glassy thud,
stunned with the future still in plain view,

but you are not headed in that direction any longer.
No way to tell for certain where any new trajectory leads.

Sitting up on the tree house platform in the afternoon,
I wonder if it's better to be like these dandelions leaning

on straw-thin stalks, no resemblance to their buttery-
bright former selves. They don't know

if the next breeze might be the one. White seeds flying,
taken by the wind.

Sunday Lunch

An acorn squash, a yam, two potatoes all split in half,
baked until flesh is soft, thin crust scraped away.

Gingery steam fills the kitchen as I search for ingredients;
soon, as usual, I'm improvising.

A hot orange spatter flies out of the soup pot;
My mother at the table, our kitchen talk urgent these days.

She always made my favourite soup, a summer borscht
whenever I came home--even in winter, managed to find

sorrel and savory.   Before her chemotherapy began,
the doctors outlined the effects and her chances in exact terms

and percentages, not factoring in the fierce spirit
that remained as her body dwindled to this thinness

that has me checking the cupboards again, trying to guess
the perfect ingredient or morsel she could not resist.

Last of all, buttermilk, just sour enough to perform
the alchemy that results in praise for flavour and shade.

I watch anxiously to see how much she has eaten, urge
one more spoonful to counteract chemicals that scald,

all of us searching for the right recipes.

The Human Scent

Her hair is still in the red bag on a shelf in the spare room.
Guests don't know--I never say here are some towels,

an extra blanket if you get cold, and this is my mother's hair
beside the board games and paperback dictionary.

She gave it to me the day after it fell out, a few weeks after
her treatments began, a week after the deer had eaten

buds from the yellow rose bush planted in August,
only spindles of stems left and too late in the season for more.

It's the human scent that keeps deer away from plants
someone had told her, and she seemed happy, as if

this solved a predicament for both of us. So why can't I
scatter her hair in the garden?

I could save a few strands the way Victorians kept a beloved's
lock in a brooch, but perhaps this bag of hair is a charm

to ward off the day when only keepsakes remain,
and tracks left by hungry deer fill in with drifting snow.

Our Fathers
(in memory of M. Boschman and J. Epp)

We muse that our fathers who art in heaven now
must be doing some kind of celestial calisthenics.
We wonder how they are keeping busy
those tightly wound fathers
who taught us how to make whistles from blades of grass,
turn summersaults and play the mandolin.

In their last years they paced, seemed anxious
to get somewhere else, their scuffling back and forth
in frayed house slippers.
Our fathers who did not spare the rod
when we were young,
who used the strap as their fathers did,
or the back of their hands, those same hands
that lifted us after falls when we were learning to walk,
that steadied us on our first two-wheelers,
and not even the accounts of their fathers' use
of corporal punishment could mend
the gaping contradiction of our father's hands.

They were awkward, our fathers' apologies
decades later when we were adults.
They handed us the raw pulp of their regret,
and we had to mold it into something
we could tuck into our pockets
along with the cold memories of punishment—
how when trying to fend off the blows
you also forsook affection
and the dappled sunlight of a summer afternoon.

It seems old-fashioned now
and I'm not sure what a buggy trace looks like,
but I've heard how one was used on my father's back,
and fists pummeled your father's shoulders and head
when the horses got out,
when he took too long leading them back.

Now when I press my ear against these stories,
I hear wind tremble leaves in a poplar bluff.
The boy's thin fingers grasp the mane of the horse,
and the breath of that horse comes
in ragged puffs,
as they both stand still on the calloused ground,
bracing for something
                    they could not stop.

Lamentable Certainties
(for mother-in-law M. Epp)

All day this quiet chittering of house finches
and juncos at the feeder.
This quiet. The chair
where you would have passed these hours.
Your oaken presence replaced by an itinerary of absence,
lamentable certainties—

you will not put on a warmer coat,
fasten each button against gusts
or reach to the back of the closet
for a woollen hat and gloves,

and you will not return your Christmas brooches
to the teak case.
Painted poinsettia and rhinestone tree
adorn the lapels of granddaughters,
who say *they're so retro*.

Your decorations will not be set back in cardboard boxes.
Dust drifts into them
on thrift store shelves.

You have joined the others
who will not walk out with us
into the new year.

These last hours of the old year mute.
I think of you again tonight
as ice crystals conceal brittle grass
and bare branches of the cherry trees
travel into moon's path,
remote as star clusters,
and closer than this breath
of the fog.

Ivy Blooming
(for father, M. Boschman)

Putting the garden to bed later than usual this year
I find hints that it never completely sleeps—
rosemary, good for memory,
still thrives on gnarled stems after summer drought.
Glint of the laurel hedge after rain,
a cage of branches at its base where a sparrow chirps
in self-imposed captivity.
Droves of bees and wasps in the alien ivy blooms.
Hearing their frenzied buzzing on a late autumn morning,
I recall how one year ago,
     father, your voice
over the phone told of an ache that led
     to a grim prognosis.
After fifty-two years of marriage and three years
of living alone, you heard
the tumor's rampant song,
it would have been nice to have had a few more years—
     your expression of regret only a courtesy.

After leaving the hospice that last time, their grief still green,
grandchildren wept outside your apartment door.
Middle-aged brothers and sisters, we entered
as if our parents had just stepped out,
folded your reading glasses,
found you had left everything in place,
the coverlet only slightly rumpled
on your side of the bed.

Gardening wisdom prescribes harsh cutting back of ivy,
but for you this morning I praise these homely globes
of pistils and stamens budding in profusion—
beloved of honeybees, beautiful to wasps.

spruce lullaby

heaving swoop of such
  heavy boughs trailing fronds,
you are not a sleek tree
  slow swinging through my days.
sweep of your lapsed greenery
  framed in the window where i need
to see you just outside the blue fence.
  droopy oldtree & at the same
time such a plush damntree,
  overgrown but i look at you
to know my cradle will be rocked.
  through swindling gusts & crush
of snow & rain splatter
  i will be rocked,
swishswung safely even if
  dangling over my stony times
even when my own momma passes
  from this earth & papa toooo
when they in alluvial rest & no more
  can i go back to talk our familiar talk
evening talk & mended clothes,
  even then i will be rocked.

i've been afraid that i will slump
  when it's time to be mighty, afraid
i will lower when it's time
  to tower when calamities that seem far
away shake the ground right below me.
  it might get harder to breathe
for me as cities fume i'll still need
  your musky exhalation, but mostly
  tonight i need tonight i need to hear
      the lull-a-bye shush
        of your darkgreen song.

So Many Winters Later

Perhaps this happened, perhaps it didn't
and in this tale I'm a pear tree
bearing a bumper crop despite drought,
my ought-to's blown away
in a scorching breeze.

And in this tale you're a crow though you rise much earlier.
Maybe you're a raven and I'll never know your mornings.
I hear only how you catechize out of your own darkness.

Much later in the day you thrash about
in branches, shaken by blustering breezes and I wonder
if I'll ever know your real genus, species,
this specious region—its cuts and draws
where hunters make a science of death.

Yet you rise much earlier
and catch the curls and crosswinds,
feathers raveled out with wear,
perched on a ridgetop

while I'm rooted in silty soil,
and difficult to know when you alight here
if you bring a ruckus or a merry diversion.
We're married in this tale
and so many winters later I scoff at magic mirrors.

This is a fable that baffles listeners,
sometimes lulls them into happily ever after
and in this tale we are lost in the forest,
sleet blurring dusk sky.
We have built a snow cave
and marvel at how its crystals conserve warmth,
but on this night, neither tree nor bird,
we're each a constellation conducting myth,
connected by thread-lines of light.

Brown Woollen Slippers

Boiled wool, heathered brown,
one half of a sheep stitched on each—
These slippers are a gift for my daughter.
These slippers are two caves.
These slippers are two rounded hills—
in old stories the ram-god disguised his consort
as a ewe, visited her on those mounds, golden
fleece, a fabric woven of sea silk, a rain cloud,
a book of alchemy.

Setting these slippers back in their membrane of tissue,
I think of the birth of my first grandchild
in five months, of this new stage not marked in my body,
of my daughter's steps tracing circles,
criss-crossing the floor at night
in brown woollen slippers.

Permission

At the end of the day
when I reach into my purse for keys,
fingers probe a soft bunched roll—
my granddaughter's folded socks,
nestled there after our visit to a berry farm.

In late spring sunlight, sky stirred with thrush song,
we plied the leafy rows, loosened red fruit
and I did not say *no*
when she could not wait to take her basket
to the tap at the field's edge,
ate strawberries seasoned with soil.
When she wanted to roll her toes in the dirt,
I agreed then collected her quickly abandoned footwear.

And at the farm store I said *yes*
when she asked for a pink glazed doughnut,
something not allowed in her house,
a foolish treat.
A taste of some long-craved permission,
a place long-parched within me
was suddenly watered with possibility.

So, now it's not difficult to imagine
this bundle could be anything—apricot, peony bud,
a small beloved bird.

Something We Would Not Name

Setting you onto the concave scale
those first weeks of anxious weighings,
grand-daughter, I called you *my rosebud, sweet peach,*
waited for the quiver of the dial to stop.
At night, the minnow quick waves
of your breath under my hand, small breaching.

So soon your legs grew sturdy, ruffled tall grass,
sent dandelion seeds afloat.

This second time rushing to the hospital,
my own legs shook as the elevator doors slid shut.
At almost two, with no resistance to a scalding
infection, its toxin spread.
I expected to find you lying in a metal bed,
but you stood clad only in a gauze vest,
while parents, nurses coaxed you to lie down.

You stood, small figure among blinking machines,
skin blistered, eyes almost swollen shut.
Arms open wide, a child in a William Blake engraving,
you reached for me, tubes trailing from your wrists,
small voice rasped--*look, I have ropes.*

In the sparse hours back home
I walked through the furnace of summer,
spikes of dry grass edging side-walks,
shrubs withering in drought.
Smoke from wild fires stung my eyes.
I passed the Italian widows
carrying their small bags of groceries.

When it was time to bring you home again,
in hushed voice the doctor urged regular doses
of medication to avoid *chasing the pain;*
and you, almost overnight, healed
and hardly seemed to recall those days

when we were all scrambling
to stay ahead of something
we would not name.

When We Found You

When I first read about the ways trees speak to one another
I thought of you, grandson, that day on the mountain—
how we were clipping into our skis, sunlight glancing
off the tiny snow mirrors, shining back up into our eyes,
perhaps blinding us
because I still don't know how we lost you.
Each of us assumed that the other was watching,
and somehow while we prepared your sled,
you vanished.

That day I raced from the warming hut to the sled hill,
from the equipment shed to the parking lot,
quick breaths of icy air drawn into the little branches
of bronchioles so I could run faster
because you were barely three years old
and there were pitiless slopes,
tree wells and strangers.
And when I feared the trees themselves might be hiding you
already telling one another about your cornflower blue eyes,
you suddenly appeared.

When we found you with too few words to tell us
why or where you wandered,
I pressed your bundled body close to mine,
my heart thudding, held my cheek against yours
as if to send an electric impulse,
to say *stay close, stay close,*
close to us.

Becoming a Tambourine
(for granddaughter, Edie)

I was once a girl beguiled by clatter of metal disks
and rambunctious thuds,
and although I wanted one of my own,
I never did get a tambourine.
Humble drum that could be grasped by any hand,
percussion instrument of children, young girls.
On ancient pottery they can be seen
holding those discs aloft or striking them
against coltish legs and burgeoning hips.

Now this girl, only four years old,
so fills my world with cheerful noise
that even on the darkest winter afternoons,
I become the timbrel.
My skin, a sounding membrane,
absorbs the romp
and frolic,
and I am tuned once more to such larks
my jangles shimmer.

This, my song, is an old song of common joy
that vibrates in those hollows of loss,
the splintered frame,
and these, my very own ribbons,
stream and spangle in the procession.

PART TWO-

Unsparing Season

"Pray for the wakeful house,
friend, and the lit window."

from *Insomnia* ~Marina Tsvetaeva

A Season's Worth

The plastic surgeon's hand glides towards my face,
Smooth knuckles adorn the slender length
of his fingers, each one delicate as a young bamboo shoot.
His Chinese name has been anglicized, but nothing
could mar the charm of these hands.
He makes a sketch of my face, includes a small black dot
beside my right eye.
Not possible to schedule me for surgery anytime soon.

Those hours distant when days melted together.
From early morning through afternoon golden
light splashed across wheat fields, gardens.
My brothers' scalps turned pink under brush-cuts,
criss-cross pattern of bathing suit straps
on my back when I returned to school.
At harvest time farmers wore a season's worth
of sun—bronze-brown that stopped
half-way up their foreheads, their two-toned arms.

Now my car caught in the snag of rush-hour traffic,
I think of holes above the clouds that will not mend,
picture the beautiful hands cutting
for hours at a time, scalpel glinting as it pries away
cells over-ripe with those long-ago summers.

Northern Iconography

On television news a boy with mesh-cap securing sutures,
and another who now calls the valiant dog his guardian.
The photo of the cougar startles most--
head surprisingly small against red-marbled snow,
paws curled back tenderly toward its chest,
an interrupted embrace.

The camera doesn't capture a child asleep, lamp left on,
and the other boy whose legs twitch beneath log cabin quilt.
Golden retriever convulsed--perhaps pinned once more,
stitches traced beneath disinfected fur.
The brave officer's pistol snug in its leather holster,
only his snores snipe into shadows.
A mother's shoulders adrift against a muslin ridge,
rows of tiny hairs still standing sentinel in her ears.

Supply Chain

My father took his own measure of the storm
over the radio crackling out a weather forecast.
His warnings—how nature could be merciless
to stragglers, the foolhardy.
His stories—gripping a rope
that connected house to barn
because livestock still had to be fed, cows milked.
Stern warnings to amuse ourselves—
yo-yo trick of the morning,
reading *Little House on the Prairie*,
still believing those land-hungry settlers
had moved to unoccupied territory.
Hours mounded up indoors
while snow clotted on window ledges.
Neighbors' houses smudged out.
Blur of caragana hedge.

When the blizzard had spent itself,
my mother made a list
and I put on snow-pants and parka,
then tucked the scrap of paper into my pocket.
The last storm clouds sulked in a grey sky.
Too soon for snowplows, only unbroken white
and drifts crested up against sheds.
I waded out alone, imagined I was an explorer,
firmly planted each footfall.

Little warmth inside the store on Main Street.
The lone clerk *said looks like your Mom is going to make
her apple sauce cake—*
four apples, a pound of butter, a quart of milk.
I had no idea how much she needed this job,
this woman who assembled items on a battered counter,
placed groceries in a brown paper bag
and handed it to me with a wink.
A widow with three sons,
one who hit the bottle early, crashed the farm truck.

Her inheritance—
rusting wire fences, a few chickens,
years to scrimp.

I had scant knowledge, too, of the decade of dust
that lingered in reminiscences—
my school-teacher grandparents
with no pay cheque for months.
I had only a slight notion of rickets,
the bare necessity of root cellar, cold storage.

On the way home,
I listened to the chittering of chickadees
and nuthatches that had stored seeds
long before we started shoveling out.

A Tracery

And the more souls who resonate together,
The greater the intensity of their love,
And, mirror-like, each soul reflects the other.
~ Dante Alighieri

Where are they now? Not in those hushed houses,
the ones that weeping relatives say they cannot bear to enter.
Dust drifts indifferently on teapots, toys and photographs—
all the things that don't add up to a life
but make a terrible claim on the living
for whom the words *intolerable, grievous*
are deep shadows of separation,
and *mother, father, sister, brother, son, daughter*
are tatters they still wrap around themselves.
Replayed on the news for days
a green explosion in the night sky,
and now thousands of miles away this city
is part of the debris field.

Between storm fronts a space opens
for remembrance, a vigil is held.
He would want me to be strong, like him,
a twelve-year old son declares,
his bearing upright for one so young.

Snow ivories the crooks of tree limbs,
and the hieroglyphs of bird tracks on a fence rail
will soon melt away.
At dusk, a tracery of branches
reflected in a window across the street—
those who so suddenly vanished are still nearby,
their lives shine back here,
even in this lamentable season of loss.

La Casa Gelato, April 2020

Though the awning above these bubble-gum-coloured walls
still proclaims *238 Flavours on Location,*
now a metal barricade is drawn over our indulgence.
I recall summer nights—
families flocking in front of display cases,
giddy kids up way past bedtime,
couples nuzzling one another's necks,
while grandparents shuffled to
o bella, ciao! bella, ciao! bella, ciao, ciao, ciao!
All that licking, sampling and so much gladness
gathered in a pink embrace, *let me taste yours*
the refrain of the place,
while white-aproned servers
dispensed small portions of possibility
on tiny spoons.

To no one I whisper *gelato*—those three opulent syllables.
How a sugary orb floats closer to parted lips,
the coldsweet second
then icy slippage as tongue and throat join the revelry,
but I taste only regret for my hesitation,
the times when I wanted to try a new flavour
—Spanish Saffron or Gorgonzola and Garlic—
but stuck with Maple Walnut.

Jasmine Plum would be perfect, I think,
as I pass by this shuttered threshold
on a pandemic afternoon,
its confections unattainable
behind the grey corrugated door.

Then with choices shrinking every day,
I head home to the savour
of solitary dusk.

Newsreel

Some days my mind can trudge no further through headlines,
bolts its doors even to statistics, sterile and blameless.
On those days, the fruity waft of banana bread,
a book on my lap or just the staccato of the kitchen clock
fills the inchoate hours at home.
No need for the scrub and lathering on coming in,
blotting chapped hands that rest,
nesting bowls in my lap.

Other days my attention flits from radio and television
to internet—the endless newsreel feeding on this affliction that lays
siege to lungs,
unaccountably sneaks into brain or heart,
pilfers lives around the globe.
Reports of the predicable up-tick in thefts
from shuttered stores.

Today it is the faces of the deceased in Nova Scotia,
after an unthinkable rampage, now the ransacked lives.
In photos and videos, a teacher's sweater
still hangs over her chair,
a young woman plays her fiddle for a virtual kitchen party,
a nurse posts a selfie at the end of her shift.
All of them gone.
Family and friends unable to reach out to offer consolation,
their hands now know a new kind of emptiness.

From my window I watch lone passersby clutch small bags
of provisions,
some wearing blue gloves—
so suddenly aware of our serviceable hands,
those extremities,
and what we could give
or take away from one another.

Front Porch

I learn how to plump up my hours,
trace the shiver of a leaf, a petal drift,
here nestled amongst my books,
sipping coffee by the window
I watch a cat creep
over a roof-top across the street,
recall how I travelled to distant cities,
ambled with others
along cobblestone streets, sniffed at the centuries-
old dust in the cathedral
before it sent cinders into night sky.

I tasted pink-fleshed shrimp on a beach,
at my feet waves lapping.
Licking, devouring the delicious world.

Now this apartment I often left, suitcase in hand,
must be *café* and *musée*,
but today it's my rambling shack in the woods.

Robins nest in its rafters,
the fledglings' insistent hunger—
beaks open even before their eyes,
and I've become the tired hound that sprawls here,
lays its head down on the splintered planks
of the front porch.

Highway 16, After Buying Supplies

The world ice-blasted.
A white crust conceals road signs.
Each small town we pass
a moment of loneliness
that presses against my chest.

Grey horse in a field.
Two more shelter by a shed.
No standing still now—
swirl of snow and cold,
we know the distance we must travel.

When you speak
I hear a dialect of winter:
terminal moraine,
ridges of glacial debris,
sky a hushed shade of lament.

Just past the last town
lies an overturned snow-plough.

Silence between us.

For miles now we have known
there is no chance of rescue.

People Also Ask

Is poetry really *the achievement of the synthesis of hyacinths and
biscuits*?
What kind of **biscuits**? Can these **biscuits** be frozen?
I have a small family and we only use three or four **biscuits** at a time.
What equipment do I need for **bird watching**?
Do **birds** somehow know when they're becoming extinct?
Does anyone have a **knitting pattern** for a sweater with an image of
Stonehenge?
Is it necessary to use **Seville oranges** to make marmalade?
Will I ever visit Seville?
What kind of glue should we use for **wallpaper**?
We live in a tiny tinder box and are thinking of **repapering**
the bedroom.
Is it true that looking at pictures of people **hugging**
can be a substitute for actual **hugging**?
Is it okay to **hug** if we use a plastic barrier sheet with arms wrapped
in cellophane and duct tape?
Will this traumatize our grandchildren?
What are you supposed to think about when **meditating**?
How can I tell if I did the **meditation** correctly?
What is the difference between gentle ***rejuvenation*** and mild hysteria?
What's causing this **pain** on my left side that moves to the right
and sometimes engulfs my entire chest?
Am I okay?
I dreamt that I was watching my own **dreams** at a drive-in theatre,
dead birds with pins stuck in them falling around me, the spherical
wailing of saws coming through the speakers.
Is there **someone** there—a benevolent gardener where we sow our
questions in the plastic plots of our computer screens,
someone who blesses our fallen
loaf of bread, toenail fungus, offer to deliver groceries?
If so, will you drive by my house?
Please don't honk, just wave and wait to see if I wave back.

***The quotation "Poetry is the synthesis of hyacinths and biscuits" from Carl
Sandberg's poem *Ten Definitions of Poetry***

All We Could Do

Perhaps years from now
when I empty the green metal watering can
at the trunk of the weeping pussy willow tree
I planted that autumn
when many like me sought simple consolations,
wore baggy clothes,
inhaled the yeasty aroma of bread,
wound skeins of wool,
I'll recall how the tree barely fit in my car
but I hauled it home,
gouged open the ground and knew
that the earth was gaping with fresh mounds.

Then as winter closed in, I waited for the silvery tufts
that protect early blooms from cold,
and how I wept
when I could not stroke
the soft heads of grandchildren,
knowing I was not the only one with a tendril of hope
and a metaphor to hold onto
in that season
when all we could do
was wait.

Springtime Diary, 2022

In late February, buds are still brown nodes
on tree branches.
A few weeks later, witness the opening
of these solar collectors, vital oxygen factories.
They are small green flags unfurled, their only anthem—
breathe,
breathe.
Breath is sacred.

Recall homely flower bulbs planted in fall,
their peeling brown papery tunics.
Marvel that they hold within them
the parrot and rainbow tulips.
Now in March they are variegated clusters commingling.

In springtime sift the soil,
witness earth's ceaseless, diurnal cycle—
the web of fungi, protozoa, and micro-anthropoids.
Find evidence of earthworm labour—
burrowing, composting.
See the bent necks of germinating seeds,
how they invoke a benediction of sunlight and rain.

And just when all this growth seems unstoppable,
a storm unleashes sleet, shivers crocuses with snow.
Like the ravages of war,
tyrant winds threaten to blight our leafy hopes,
even while many of us are ready to restore this earth
pocked and poisoned by battles.
Wielding only plowshares and pruning hooks
we long to make scorched ground flourish.

Here at the Crux

That night I heard the wheeze of the dying season
at the windowpane of the small classroom.
Professor H.'s voice was unspooling in American Lit class,
his tweed jacket baggy and his grey ponytail
wriggling over his collar, down his back.
Our textbooks lay open—a few centuries of words,
heavy in spite of the flimsy pages
on which most students added only light pencil marks,
hoping to resell them.

Sometimes my mind wandered
out to the edges of the city, into bluffs
where my mother planned to pick rosehips the next day
or returned to the kitchen where I had helped her
with canning that afternoon, choice fruit
brought back from the Okanagan by some neighbour,
but she could make the best of runty crab apples
or chokecherries.

As we discussed imagery and symbolism,
I thought how simple her creations—
fruit, water, sugar, thickened with pectin.
Those jars lined up on the counter,
inside peaches suspended with small hollows
where the pits had been,
syrup turned to amber in the scant light of the rangehood.
Gardens and fields had recently brimmed over
where less than a century ago
dust smothered the hopes of our grandparents.

I watched the tip of Professor H.'s cigarette glow,
tried to guess if sparks would fall
before he could flick them into the portable ashtray
with its checkered beanbag base
which he routinely set on the desk
before he started the class.
He was flapping his arms around more than usual,
a slight hunch to his back as he paced.

We were discussing *The Grapes of Wrath,*
jostling to catch the questions he tossed at us.

When he read the last scene aloud—
Rosasharn, her baby dead,
offering her milk to the starving man—
the guys smirked and young women blushed,
glanced downwards.
I wondered at the very idea of that emaciated man
looking up at me like that,
the shadowed craters of his face,
imagined the cracked lips
and his taking me into his dry mouth.
Needing me to live.

Silence after Professor H. stopped reading,
all hoping he wouldn't ask us to comment,
but he stared down at the page,
suddenly slumped and began to sob.
Finally, he managed to say that mythology was powerful,
but it wouldn't change anything if we couldn't grasp it.
Shakily, he lit another cigarette,
said his family was convinced
he was having a mid-life crisis.
Someone raised their hand, politely asked if that were true.
He laughed, and matter of factly said
No, I've probably always been batshit crazy.

Now when my students sneak glances at their cellphones
or drift into laptop screens, at times I, too, want to cry.
Every day more stories of desperate migrants,
floods, and wildfires.
My mother's ashes settling in a distant plot,
her yellowing recipe cards rarely taken out of the metal box
at the back of a cupboard.
Grief here at the crux of my life
where it could all go down in cinders and soot.
Dust piling up on window ledges again.

Lowland

Don't stop—
that destiny-wracked voice inside me whispered,
my fingers clutched the steering wheel
as I swerved around bloated puddles
on the side of the highway
and boulders that tumbled before the mudslides.
I'm certain we heard the groan of drenched soil,
night's moan.

Lit only by our headlamps, the sky was a river
more swollen than those we skirted
—Similkameen, Tulameen, Fraser—
on our way back to the coast.

The next morning's news:
swamped cities, severed roadways,
valleys turned to lakes.
Lives engulfed by flood waters,
travellers missing.
A lowland of grief.
Roots that could have held back the water
rotting in clear-cuts,
or burned away in wildfires.

And on that first morning of lost moorings
people began to send messages
about those who needed shelter, food.
They ferried tins of infant formula,
woolen toques, pillows,
second-hand comforters.
They went out in boats
to tether cattle, deliver medicine.
Some sailed over thickets,
over thousands of dead animals
lying among marrowy stumps,
submerged depth-gauges,
in this unsparing season we've created.

storm system

with dwindling provisions
you navigate another drenched morning,
your house an ark in an alien season.
this winter one storm system after another,
and when you step out onto the deck
for the jolt of negative ions
that ruffles the dead space around your brain
you're greeted by the whirring of miniature wings
by the feeder you faithfully bring in the house each night.
that's when you hear him—
you can't tell exactly in which yard
but nearby a man is groaning loudly,
not the quick spasm of solar plexus
when lifting something heavy, but a moan torn from gut
that is morphing into a bellow.
in a rain shadow of raw grief it's suddenly not possible
to walk back inside. this man weeps
as though he has just stepped away from a deathbed,
his, the crying of someone who is mourning a lost lover,
a lost world. crying that makes you wonder
if this is the tsunami of sorrow
that causes someone to pick up a rifle
and rooted there you notice the cracks in the wall
below the eaves where the exterminator sprayed
poison in the spring, *no choice, really*, he said,
carpenter ants can demolish your house.

too early to know if they'll return.
hard to predict the trees now, too—
bare branches where there was a plum frenzy
just a few months before and brown stalks of a shrub
that didn't survive drought, dry nubs of mint flowers
you hoped would attract bees and each morning
your own hummingbird thirst
now offered only someone else's cedared darkness.
and yet you find his sobs saturating the air are not strange,
this weeping man is not really
a stranger.

Mid-winter Reading List

Tsvetaeva's words taste of cinders,
imploded years.
Each line a ladle—come sip here,
            night drifter, fellow migrant,
outlast these famine months.

A musty songbook bought for only pennies
            at a bazaar.
Tonight my own song drowned out by raven
on a stark limb of arbutus—
            Tsvetaeva's black-eyed child crying.

A list of flowers for an extinct perfume:
small whorled pogonia, drooping trillium,
thread-leaved sundew.
Ask: what else may have vanished
by the end of the year?

Invitation to a banquet:
candles snuffed at midnight,
wisps of winter's fables float out the window.
Far in the back, a table set
for those whose inheritance is dust.

Quick, find a birthing guide—
all of us in this passageway together.
Devise a language
to paraphrase these nascent hours
after we are brought forth
to this solstice sunrise.

(Marina Tsvetaeva—Russian poet b. 1892, committed suicide 1941)

PART THREE

Sing Only of Return

"Everything is plundered, betrayed, sold,
Death's great black wing scrapes the air,
Misery gnaws to the bone.
Why then do we not despair?"

from *Everything is Plundered, Betrayed, Sold*
~Anna Akhmatova

The Outfield

Caught daydreaming again in the outfield as a fly-ball soars
its steep arc, then bounces at her feet--
always the second too late scrabble, always last picked player.
Tree-climber, peering into a nest of perfect blue ovals,
splattered on the basketball court by big girls.
Daughter of a track and field coach, still teased about her terror
of the high jump bar, how she screeched to a stop in mid-stride
like a cartoon character, arm thrown up to shield her face.
Champion of skipping PE, scrawled poems in notebook margins.

Pyramids rise in corners of the gym, grey weights stacked
like steel sonnets, ballad stanzas, compact couplets.
She uses breath to heft them.
Women and men, same rows of muscle, gnarl of cartilage,
amplified shoulders, flesh of breasts receding.
Mostly, she recognizes the way they sit in silence before the hoist
and clank of metal that glints above their heads,
just as she sits a long time before setting down a single line.

Introduction to Philosophy: Classical and Contemporary Readings

I thought the textbook could be salvaged
after it resided with a rotting apple in my backpack,
and even after it was drenched by autumn rainfall
on the porch where I had set it to air out.
But after a rat made it the main course
of its evening meal,
I knew for certain I would never
taste those last few chapters.

I took consolation from the fact
we had both savoured its lexicon,
and it was true
some of those words for me
had been like the hot burst of a radish
on my tongue.

The book still lies on its sodden front cover,
holes chewed out of its back.
Small tatters of paper lie scattered about—
the less digestible parts, I suppose,
and I find myself wondering if the rat most enjoyed
The Mind-Body Problem,
or if it preferred the blandness of
Stoic Resignation to Fate.

The Match

On that first day of class,
when students shared career goals and hobbies,
he didn't elaborate when he said
Mixed Martial Arts.
When they made name cards,
the letters on his were taut, punched out.

Well past mid-term when I have learned their names,
he sets his card out, declares himself
still in the competition.
When he stays after class,
each question is spring-loaded.
He vigilantly seeks out the place
where I might out-manoeuvre him.
But I resist thinking of myself as an opponent;
more of a referee, I remind them of due dates,
assignment late policies, penalties for plagiarism.

On a late fall afternoon
when light leaks through metal blinds
and the only sound is an occasional sigh,
he attacks the in-class composition, jaw set firm.
At the half-way point, he takes off the black baseball cap
that has shaded his eyes all semester,
revealing a blonde bristle of hair.
Suddenly, he looks no more than twelve years old
and I can't imagine kicks to this face,
knees to the ribcage, hammer fists to his chest.

When he quickly picks up his pen,
sinews lace his hand.
By now the others are shuffling,
shaking their forearms.
When they have grappled with grammar and syntax
for long enough, I call time.

After the semester has been clinched
by the submission of final grades,
the manila envelope full of course evaluations
arrives in my mail slot.
In the midst of scanning ticked boxes,
I am halted by his comment—
Thanks for everything. I really liked your class.

He has signed his name, drawn a happy face beside it.
And I, momentarily stunned,
think how well he hid his liking,
then quickly overcome my loss
of balance.

Sylvia Plath on the North Coast

i.   If I meet you tonight on the blunt-edged
Rocks and we walk hand in hand to the sea,
Stare down the stars,
Will I be swept away in the surge and up-
Rising of uneasy words?
A trove of curses, this voice that wants

To wail its way out of my throat.

ii.   I see you admire the stitches here, flagrant
Green this night-
Dress of kelp, strands that trail salt,
Tearing squalls, cold moon a witness.

How I've tried to leave you behind, my darkling
Girl entranced in these night dances.

iii   No billow of linen triangle or squat row boat
Pulled alongside.
Not your style.
O siren, again you stalk
Patch over your eye, your sharp-edged
Consonants against my throat and me offering
No resistance.

iv   Five nights in a row you breached
The surface and I placed my hand on that slick
Below the keyholes of your eyes that saw
So far below, but I could not go with you
As before, the line tied round my ankle,

Tonight I cut the cord.

Heritage/Language

Pautsche (to patter noisily through puddles),
a word that slipped out of memory's pocket
more than forty years ago
until a spring walk reminded me
as a pebble withholds particles of earth after water
and in late summer river stones recall
a gurgling lullaby.

For days I am lost between pages
or absorbed in the flickering screen
and forget to replace hummingbirds' nectar,
but faithful they return even after weeks.

Small whirring verbs,
they tip their heads back and do not ponder
absence or presence.

Cherry tree boughs frilled with blossom now
and bees swarm in *Himmelblieu,*
sweet orbs will form here
and who would think of bare limbs or departures
when April's birds sing only of return.

The door opens backwards into retrieval,
into gratitude for these words,
these pages a reunion,
each faint notebook line a horizon
that cannot contain everything,
the last loop, each fading black dot,
even the space that follows
overflows with possibility.

Spelling Lessons

When I first grasped those marvelous shapes called letters
conjured my name, spelled me,
I took hold of the fat red pencil,
traced them over and over in scrapbooks, on walls,
later on the blackboard, and on paper
still ripe with scent of the spirit duplicator.
Journals were filled with them,
stories tapped out on an electric typewriter;
then poetry resided in the square plastic hulk
of my first computer.

Reading the poems of Emily Dickinson,
I sometimes pictured her sister Lavinia
finding the box beneath the bed
after the poet was gone, her verses handwritten
on stationery, stitched together.

Reading those verses I, too,
could unfold the inscrutable bundles
with their script of letters and dashes
scattered like foot-prints
of small birds,
I could release
that *certain slant of light.*

Later, all those hours spent in grey classrooms
learning that those marks were only empty signifiers.

For a time,
the incantations of favourite childhood tales
were muted,
the slant of light splintered,
but it was never put back into the box.

Prescription

The doctor said time alone would ease
these winter ailments, now spring temperatures
unseasonably low.
But there was something more virulent slinking
through my capillaries, sticky thoughts,
chronic doubts, like coughing fits that left me weak.
More difficult each morning to leave
   the cave of sleep.

According to black birds, this condition isn't fatal.
The way crows soar their darkness,
                  then settle on the lightest boughs.
Ravens, their raucous songs, gurgling
up from the crossflow of moans,
                        shrieks
of laughter.

A consultation at twilight, they prescribed the cure—
   chants accompanied by clinking of chimes
made of sea glass, rusty nails, and water
   sloshed in discarded calabashes.
Prayers to be intoned while thumbing
   a rosary of agates, marmot bones, and emeralds.

Now I savour each sip of cottonwood
sap that reaches me from the river's bed, each wave
of sunlight that crashes through the window
             knocking everything to the floor,
   while dark wings flap overhead.

Never Too Late

*"She's not the fastest and she's not the strongest but she is willing
to stick with it for a long, long time and just keep grinding."*
 -Alex Honnold describing his mother Dierdre Wolownick,
   oldest woman to summit El Capitan on her 70th birthday.

First, hike through giant sequoias, stands of hemlock
and lodgepole pine, then clamber over boulders
following the Merced River to the base.
Looking up it's not possible to see the summit of El Capitan,
face to face with a three-thousand-foot granite monolith,
an igneous-streaked grimace gives nothing away
unless you count the frequent rockfalls
that take out interlopers,
or see it as one climber did—
a building wave looming above you.

Here's a safer viewpoint—
countless photos taken at sunset from far down the valley
feature a bright angular patch of orange light
above the dead grey granite below.
In one photo, clouds froth around the summit
catching that last light, creating an illusion
of lava and flames,
but the entire structure is the inner core
of an ancient volcano.

When she started climbing,
Dierdre said she just wanted to get closer to her son,
the famous one always shinnying up mountains
around the world.
After a lengthy career of teaching languages,
she wanted to understand his vocabulary—
quickdraw, *jugging*, and *trad*.
So, at sixty, referring to herself as *a lumpy old mom*,
she began to go to the gym.

The first time she climbed El Capitan
took thirteen hours up and six back down
on the Lurking Fear route.
Just walk steeply uphill, endlessly grabbing
Whatever tiny edges you can find, she advises.

Perhaps, I think, like writing poetry,
sometimes slow plodding and how it's not possible
to see the whole poem at first, but forms emerge as adjectives
and adverbs fall away.

Handholds aren't enough, of course.
Footholds are needed to stay close to the idea,
and, suddenly, there you are clinging—
tongue, breath, sinew and bone,
against the poem.

Dierdre humbly offers herself up as an example
of autumnal success:
it's never too late
to start a new hobby.

Then she describes the risks of falling
on that first day of her 70th year:
I'd roll down slab after slab, breaking parts of me at every bump
of rock, until I reached the edge. Then I'd sail out over the Valley
to plummet down 3,200 feet to the Valley floor.

Looking at a picture of El Capitan
I contemplate a new hobby and decide for now
to reach for verbs and nouns,
to put down one word after another,
to just keep grinding
across the page.

Wild Turkeys

Besides their small heads, bulky bodies,
and scaly straws for legs,
they don't match—
some have blue-tinged faces, others red.
And what the hell are those things
growing out of the middle of their foreheads called?
I used to wonder when turkeys strutted
up to my front doorstep,
those small horn-like protrusions or wobbling blobs,
but I no longer need to know, don't do an internet search,
instead name one bird Google.

What's certain is that they've been out there doing it.
Hoarse squawks and bellows in the bushes—
they've reproduced.
Wild. Domesticated. Wild once more.
A neighbour said that a farmer once brought turkeys
to Vancouver Island but they flew the coop,
laid low somewhere then emerged in small flocks.
Visitors ask *are they wild, you know,*
like the original native turkey species of North America?
I simply don't know.

I'm forewarned they will mess up a garden,
or flap onto a car and flail about
scratching paint and window glass,
but they've never committed these delinquent acts
on my yard or on my watch.
They just show up once or twice a week
when I'm having a tough morning,
and because they look like something
kindergarten kids would make out of plasticene,
laughing so hard they drooled
while attaching random appendages,
wild turkeys make me smile.

With their gawky gait and low cackling reassurance
they make me smile

and never ask if I'm a run-away—
they seem to know at some time
we've all escaped from something or somewhere.
They seem to say
you there, with your weed patch of self-doubt
and overgrown brambles of grief, you belong here, too.
Just find your flock.

E & N Railway

Hewn and squared
these railway ties are splintered remnants
of schemes that proved too grand for this island,
an enterprise that once shunted through old growth forest.
Alongside Shawnigan Lake
the train no longer sways past summer cottages,
some with only a mossy lattice for a roof—
hearths exposed to rain.

Steel rails that once gleamed now keep company
with a calligraphy of curses,
declarations of love scrawled on the waiting platform
littered with bottles, cigarette butts.
Wild sweet peas, clumps of clover
overgrow the aspirations of coal barons.

I walk these tracks years after I lurched away
from that first town with my baggage of blizzards, betrayals
and a grassy fragrance of fields and prairie sage.

This track is a lakeside trail where once I heard
the most ecstatic treetop chorus
of finch, varied thrush—
arbutus a vestry for their song.

I follow this scrap of past ambitions
when almost erased by snow, lake keeps its own counsel,
and in spring trudge through cold muck
left by flood waters,
shoreline dank with cottonwood.

In late summer when sun douses rosehips
and wasps settle on beaded ooze of blackberries,
imagined itineraries are all but forgotten.

Sunday Picnics
(for Pam Sherwin)

At one end of our street
tangled branches of cedar, arbutus, honey locust
thrust above the wire fence of Acacia Manor
that keeps its inhabitants
safe from the perils of forgetting,
or remembering.

On this same street your days are still spent
in this small kitchen.
A husband's loyal ministrations—
afternoon tea and blackberry crisp.
When a name or word tumbles off the shelves of recall,
you throw back your head and laugh,
tell me again of your childhood in Wiltshire County--
Sunday picnics, lying on fallen megaliths,
sun-heated sarsen at Stonehenge.

Impossible to know beyond the eclipse of centuries
what was worshipped there.
With no concern for misplaced bric-a-brac of memory,
you recollect giants, their lichen-dappled heads
rising up into outspread sky dotted with blackbirds.

After this whirl of words, what occupies your silence?
Perhaps a still warm imprint on your back,
you listen to what archeologists, doctors,
even a husband cannot hear—
ancient whispers in stone.

A Blessing
(for Sherry Small)

At *Hoobiyee**, a celebration in the heart of the city,
far from my friend's Northern home,
a large canvas crescent Moon and Star were suspended
from the ceiling of the old PNE hall–
portend of an ample harvest of berries and salmon.
When the final dance of the night began
people moved down the worn bleachers
in a way that was both casual and dignified
and I suddenly felt remote from where my own
ancestors had started out,
or where they had set down on land
that was handed to them
after they had lost their homes somewhere else,
but two wrongs didn't make a right.
So, when that last dance began I wanted to stay in my seat
but because my friend had asked me to join her,
I made my way to a place
where I was carried in the current.
All our feet moving to the clack and boom of drums.

I want my words to be as accurate as possible
when I describe the flow and surge, call and response,
the step then wait of that crowd.
No matter where it moved there was a centre
and when swan's down was blown up into the air–
it drifted like glistening starlight
            onto the hair and shoulders
                        of the dancers,
a blessing for all to see.

*(*Hoobiyee—Nisga'a New Year)*

Forgetting

I have forgotten the entry-code to your apartment
and now on my tongue
only a faint taste of jasmine tea and persimmons
from that first night
we stayed up until dawn.

That first night I told you about the war,
my grandmother's stories of fleeing,
my sister who forgot our grandmother's spell
for releasing wandering spirits
and how we stopped our sleep-walking brother
from leaving the house.

Forgetting is a blessing, a trance,
this slipping from memory,
this lingering in the hallway,
and on the other side of the door of forgetting
are deserted battlefields, beloved brothers,
small white jasmine petals unlocking musky fragrance
and the honeyed skin of fruit
that will never taste as sweet again.

North Coast Devotional

At the edge of the land
transient souls take shelter in autumn,
gather in a longhouse built in the old way—
sturdy cedar posts, spiring roof.
At first shy devotees who want
to intone our way through long nights.
Radiant verses from many faiths sustain us
through the rain-drenched north coast winter.

Charles, seven-feet tall, cycles in down-pours,
a conga and doumbek tied to his bicycle.
He fashions a drum from an old propane tank,
paints on it a lotus,
an instrument for yearning spirits—
its timbre set to our *Om Mani Padmi Hum.*

Dagmar offers ancient earth chants from Estonia,
asks us to chant in an old munitions bunker
built during World War II.
She brings a candelabra
and five stormproof candles.
Our voices chorale together in that place,
harmonize where weapons once were heaped.

With the greening of the earth
in springtime our voices so close,
it's difficult to tell whether notes heard
are our own or another's.

One ting of a small brass bell
calls us together,
a drumbeat pulses
in the shrine of a single ribcage.

East Pender Street Diary

Mrs. Hill, the neighbor in #3, told me Helen lived here for almost forty years, how they watched Wheel of Fortune together except for two evenings a week when Charlie from #8 came down to play poker. Helen's days were spent at this second-floor window; she didn't even go down for the summer picnic—Mrs. Hill brought her a leg of chicken and potato salad on a checkered plate. When they carried her out at ninety-seven, lungs festering with pneumonia, Helen swore she'd be back.

Autumn drafts rattle these windows, their mottled aluminum frames, loose handles. Weeks after moving in, I still think of this place as Helen's apartment. A grey mound of curtains in a corner, the only thing here when I moved in. But apparently Helen didn't care who looked in, saw her in a fraying housecoat. This morning I wonder if the faux fireplace mantle is really a left-over wish for warmth to gather around but from what I've heard, Helen wasn't overly sociable. She was practical, could recognize a deal—four decades of below market rent and someone to sit with when the pipes started to rattle and the circuits corroded. When that wheel was spun, she was a winner.

It's already December and just before leaving on winter vacation, a tapping at my door—the landlord with an amicable smile drops off a bottle of maple syrup and a Christmas card. Suddenly, I see again the line of cards my mother strung up in the kitchen each year—snow-bound villages, gift-filled sleighs, nativities, cheerful benedictions from one home to another, the looping contour of each distinct signature.

Send me a card, Helen, from wherever you are now—out of the country, no need for sturdy luggage. Most of your life was lived in the last century with its baggage of wars, weapons of mass destruction, headlines like *Senator lives—Blonde dies*. In the bedroom, your dreams still drift like strands of hair I find between floorboards. When I awaken sometimes it seems there is just a room between and it isn't a flea-market hall full of mid-century tableware and ornaments, the pretty-girl vases with hollow heads where the flowers go. Who thought of that?

While waiting for yours to arrive, I will send you a newsy card—I see children head off to school. They bounce like leaves buoyed by a spring breeze, but on the evening news I've heard them talk about making plans just in case they must rescue one another from a shooter. A few weeks ago, a young woman barricaded in a hotel room sent out messages to the world, a desperate supplicant hoping that someone would answer like certain trees do after a cold winter. Even just a few amber drops.

Pale light of early spring on a February afternoon, but I'm fairly certain, Helen, that seasons no longer concern you—no need for mothballs between sweaters entombed in cedar chests or freshening up summer linens. After a long, slow tumble now you float in a fifth season, that umbilical vine severed that connected you to the nubby belly of earth. I don't know your birthday, but twelve months to measure time seems meagre. You can be a birthday girl every day now. I like to picture you in your housecoat floating on a bamboo raft on a sea of supernovas.

I remember once as a child being afraid when I couldn't see my parents. Sitting stiffly on my aunt's sofa, staring out her window, I willed them to walk through the door. Not long ago on an evening the first winter after they were both gone, just before Christmas I went to the cemetery, a maple tree the only landmark in the darkness but no way to find their headstone, the ground rippled white. How close they felt in that holy hush. Now just beyond our window, Helen, I see the swollen tips of branches. They can only hold the light in for so long before they burst open.

Morning Fog

***"The troubles of this world pass, and what we have left
is what we have made of our souls." -Shoghi Effendi***

I

Morning's soft shoe shuffle out
of slumber
push away the duvet
awaken to a world sheathed
in fog.

Not gauze or linen,
silk comes closer,
a slip-covered world,
day's immaculate coverlet.

How mountains acquiesce,
become silhouette,
a dialect of hush
the eyes understand and know
no touching the mystery
behind the silver-tinged veil.

II

These mornings
I wonder what I am
inside this fog,
what part of me is fog?

Part of me is fog—
call it breath, patience,
threshold.

Fog whispers
here is your answer,
hear how particles of prayers
hover.

What I am making
of my soul—
a first shearing,
lambs' wool
winding a skein
knowing all you've gathered
will be unraveled.

Tiny glass seed beads of light
on the lake,
each sequined gesture
towards love
pure shearling
sacred undyed
yearning to be tinged
by prismatic devotion.

III

Troubles of this world pass
the rowers
soon out of sight.
What is left is this
soul-shaping
artisan-ship of liquid
stratus hovering
over the lake
at this dewpoint
of my day.

Acknowledgments

I wish to thank poet friends and members of writing groups for their input on many of the poems in this collection. In particular, I am grateful for the reading and comments of the A-Drift Writers Collective (Christopher Levenson, Adrienne Drobnies, Ken Klonsky, Bill Ellis, Nilofar Shidmehr, Robin Pacific, Tom Gorman, and the late Kieran Egan). I would also like to acknowledge that several of the poems were written in connection with events sponsored by Pandora's Writing Collective. A few of the poems had their origin in a class taught by Fiona Tinwei Lam and Evelyn Lau at Simon Fraser University and benefited from the wonderful editorial input of both instructors and classmates. Finally, I would like to thank members of the Salish Sea Writers Collective for the helpful discussions.

Some of the poems in this collection have appeared in the anthologies *Unfurled: Collected Poetry from Northern BC Women* (Caitlin Press, 2010) and *Forcefield: 77 Women Poets of British Columbia* (Mother Tongue Publishing Limited, 2013). *Brown Woollen Slippers* originally appeared in the chapbook *Nothing But Sound and World* published by Leaf Press. As well, some of these poems have appeared in the Canadian journals Room Magazine, Island. Writer Magazine, and The Temz Review, as well as the Berlin-based journal The Wild Word. *Hymns for Sad Ballads* won the first-place poetry prize in the Delta Literary Arts 2022 Poetry Contest. Both *Midwinter Reading List* and *Forgetting* became the texts for art songs that can be heard at artsonglab.com